MELISSA DI DONATO ROOS

ILLUSTRATED BY ANGE ALLEN

How Do Mermaids Poo?

novum ◆ premium

www.novum-publishing.co.uk

© 2021 novum publishing

ISBN 978-3-99107-347-5
Editing: Hugo Chandler, BA
Cover design, layout & typesetting: novum publishing
Cover, internal illustrations: Ange Allen

www.novum-publishing.co.uk

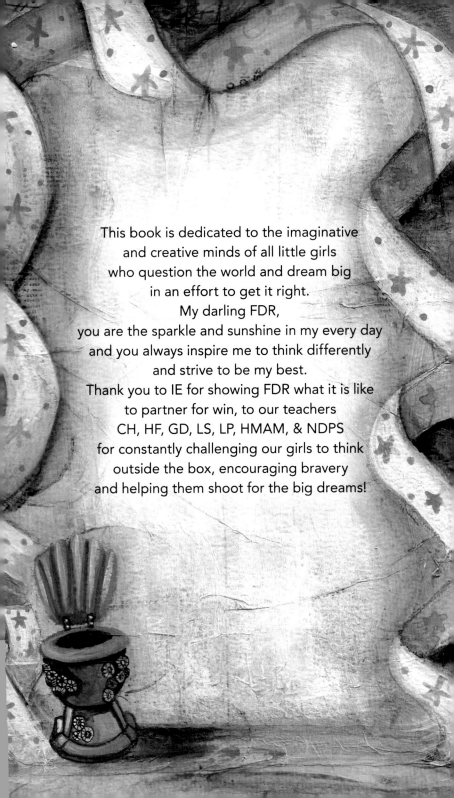

This book is dedicated to the imaginative
and creative minds of all little girls
who question the world and dream big
in an effort to get it right.
My darling FDR,
you are the sparkle and sunshine in my every day
and you always inspire me to think differently
and strive to be my best.
Thank you to IE for showing FDR what it is like
to partner for win, to our teachers
CH, HF, GD, LS, LP, HMAM, & NDPS
for constantly challenging our girls to think
outside the box, encouraging bravery
and helping them shoot for the big dreams!

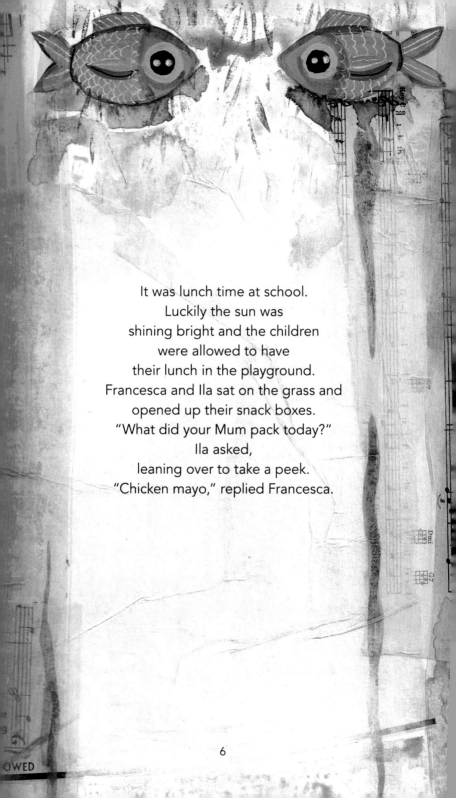

It was lunch time at school.
Luckily the sun was
shining bright and the children
were allowed to have
their lunch in the playground.
Francesca and Ila sat on the grass and
opened up their snack boxes.
"What did your Mum pack today?"
Ila asked,
leaning over to take a peek.
"Chicken mayo," replied Francesca.

"I've got cheese and tomato.
Francesca, do you want to swap,"
Ila suggested.
Francesca nodded.
They usually preferred one another's lunches.

Francesca then thought and asked,
"So … what's your plan for
our fantasy poem assignment?"
Ila wondered what she might do and replied,
"I'm not sure.
What fantasy creature are you going
to draw and write about?
I am more worried about the poem
than the drawing.
It is hard to use questions to write a poem.
This is a tough assignment!"

"Maybe a purple unicorn or a chameleon
that breathes sparkles,"
Francesca replied, "or …
actually … I think I might like
to do a mermaid."
The girls took a bite of their sandwiches.

9

Francesca began to think more about
the magic of mermaids and questioned,
"Have you ever wondered why mermaids
don't get wrinkly skin in the water,
like we do when we swim for too long?" Francesca asked Ila.
"That sometimes happens to my brother and I on summer holiday.
Or …" Ila giggled, "have you ever wondered
how they go to the toilet?
I mean, seriously, do they remove their tails or something?
How do you think mermaids poo and use the loo?"
The girls laughed out loud.
Francesca almost choked on her sandwich.
Francesca chuckled and laughed, "That's actually very funny.
Why don't we ask Miss Charris if we can do
our assignment together?
Maybe we can write our poem that tries to solve
this funny question …
'How do Mermaids Poo'?"

Together the girls worked hard on their fantasy poem project
and they were quite proud of themselves
when they handed it in.
The completed project was beautifully painted,
it was filled with great
rhymes with big questions, and all done on time.
Monday morning came around. Francesca and Ila met on the
corner of Confidence and Power Street and walked to school
together, chatting about their weekend.
As they neared school, Francesca remembered,
"Hey, we have to present our poem
project to the class today."
"I almost forgot," laughed Ila. "I hope Miss Charris likes
ours! Do you think she will get cross with us
because our poem is really silly?"
With a very worried look, Francesca replied,
"I'm not sure, but I do hope we don't end up in trouble."

The school day started and the teachers came into the
playground to round up the children to start the day.
The children all raced to class.
"NO RUNNING CHILDREN!"
shouted Headmistress Pretzel."
Settle down children and Happy Monday!" Miss Charris
clapped her hands always enthusiastically,
but more so on Monday mornings.
The children took their seats, feeling a little nervous
about who would be called up first. Miss Charris, as usu-
al, enthusiastically began the lesson by saying, "You all
did splendidly on your fantasy poem projects but two
girls in the class came up with some intriguing questions.
These two girls formed a team and had the confidence
to ask some bold questions, which, children is one of the
greatest gifts we can give to one another."

"Francesca and Ila, please come up to the front and
read your poem to the class.
I'll hold up your art while you read."
The girls walked to the front of their class
and Francesca spoke first.
"For our assignment, we chose to paint mermaids.
We had a few questions that we found a bit funny,
so we wrote our poem about them too.
Ila will read it to you."
Ila cleared her throat and began, "How do Mermaids Poo?
by Ila and Francesca."
The class erupted into fits of laughter.
Miss Charris could not hold in her giggle either.
She put her hand in front of her mouth.

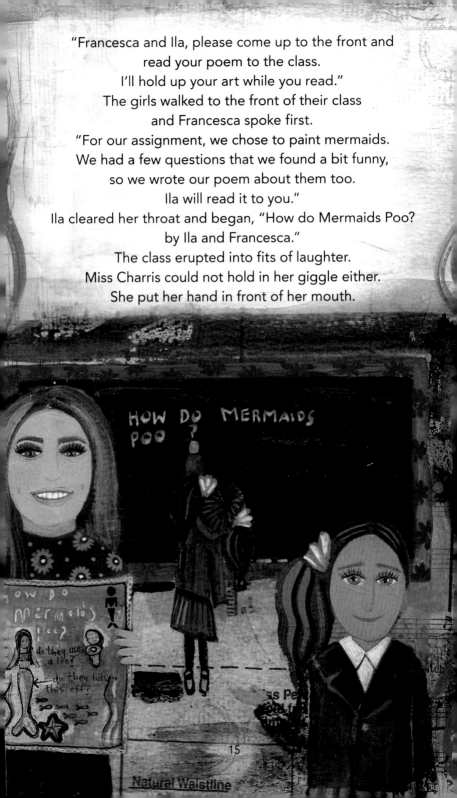

Ila cautiously started the poem …
"How do mermaids use the toilet?
It is hard to imagine, and we don't want to spoil it.
Does a hole magically appear on their backside?
Do they need to come ashore during low tide?
How do mermaids make a poo?
Assuming of course, that they have no loo.
Do they grow a pair of legs and walk out of the sea?
Do they dig a hole in the sand to have a wee?"

"Does it leak from their sparkly scales?
This doesn't get taught in our fairy tales.
If they have no bum,
what do they do with a rumbling tum?
Does it drip from the very end of their tail?
Who might know, a fish, a dolphin or maybe a whale?
So next time you swim in the sea,
I know what your very first thought will be …
Where is the 'sea loo'
so that mermaids have a place to poo?"

The class had been desperately
trying to hold in their laughter.
They knew better than to interrupt a presentation,
but they could not keep quiet any longer.
They burst into hysterical laughter.
Miss Charris eventually had to threaten them with
extra maths homework if they didn't calm down.

Once the laughter and the clapping
subsided, Zoe raised her hand and asked,
"Miss Charris why are you not cross
with the girls for this silly poem?"
Miss Charris began to explain, "Children,
it is wonderful to question the world, isn't it!?
The world is only as big and
as magical as your imagination!"

Miss Charris continued, "Children,
question everything and allow
your mind to explore! It is like a treasure
map and the questions
are your clues that take you on the journey.
Let's hear how creative you all are!
Be confident and be bold children
with your questions, as then you may take a
treasure hunt to find amazing answers!

where
is
the
loo?

With the mermaids,
these creative questions led us on a trip
to the sea today!"

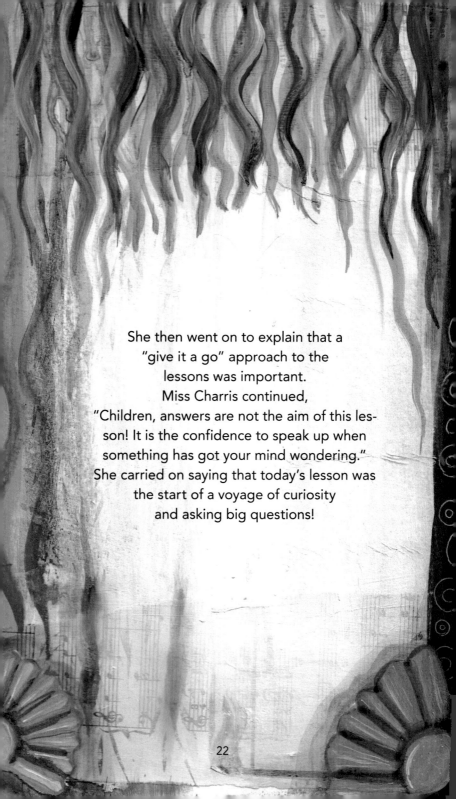

She then went on to explain that a
"give it a go" approach to the
lessons was important.
Miss Charris continued,
"Children, answers are not the aim of this lesson! It is the confidence to speak up when
something has got your mind wondering."
She carried on saying that today's lesson was
the start of a voyage of curiosity
and asking big questions!

Miss Charris added "I believe that Francesca and Ila did that perfectly in this assignment.
What do you think children?
They have the freedom of imagination!".

"Allow me to show you what I mean,"
Miss Charris enthusiastically started …
"Why is it, do you think, a mermaids skin doesn't shrink.
She spends all day in the sea,
but when I swim for too long,
something goes horribly wrong.
My toes are as wrinkly as can be!"

Roars of laughter overcame the class and
the children began to cheer.
Miss Charris continued,
"Maybe they have waterproof skin
like a seal or a dolphin?
How do mermaids brush their hair?
Is it under the water or in the open air?
Do they comb it when perched on a rock?
That's when sailors spot them and get a big shock."

"I've heard that mermaids grow legs
and walk onto land.
Do you think this is magic or perfectly planned?
Or do they actually have legs that they try to hide?
Maybe it is their slip-on tail and there are feet inside!"

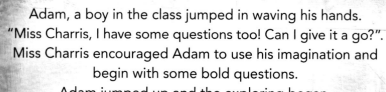

Adam, a boy in the class jumped in waving his hands.
"Miss Charris, I have some questions too! Can I give it a go?".
Miss Charris encouraged Adam to use his imagination and
begin with some bold questions.
Adam jumped up and the exploring began,
"Are mermaids afraid of sharks or do sharks run and hide?
Mermaids are clever, that can't be denied!

Do they ride on dolphins like we do on horses?
Can they sing underwater and will fish join forces?"

27

All the children jumped up and down with their
hands raised to join in on the fun.
Ren was chosen next and shouted out quickly
while laughing as she questioned,
"Do they use chairs and set tables under the sea?
Where do they eat, how could it be?"

Seaweed
Allergy!

Seaweed
Symptoms
patient
into

"What if they don't like salt on their food?
What if they are sick of swimming, and are just not in
the mood?
Can a mermaid be allergic to seaweed?
Do their fish friends know when she's wee'd?"

Miss Charris clapped encouragingly and
roared with laughter,
as did all the children in the classroom.

She turned back to Ila and Francesca, thanking
them for leading the lesson and teaching all the children
the importance of thinking differently,
questioning what they know and perhaps don't know,
and adding a little 'whizz, bang and sparkle'
to their assignment with big thinking.

Chloe raised her hand and said, "Miss Charris,
I want to know
more about mermaids,
not only about how they poo but also
how they talk! I have so many questions!"
"Of course you do, as you should Chloe.
Now that you all understand
the importance of curiosity!
Your assignment is to go home and ask your parents
if they know about mermaids!
We might just spark an enquiring mind in them too!"

The End